Eggy's Secret:
An Addie Adventure

BY

A. Fergusson

DEDICATION

For my family. You inspired me to write this story. You bring so much joy, laughter, and love! Love you always and I'm so lucky to have you all.

It all started when I was traveling with my family. We were hiking through the red rocks of Sedona, when I spotted one that looked out of place.

It was oddly smooth and had a spiral stripe on it too. It was heavy like a rock but looked like an egg. I named it Eggy.

After we returned home, I took it
everywhere with me. I became obsessed
with Eggy.. It was even in my dreams!

One day after school, I was looking out
my window as we drove home. That is
when it all changed. It was like a dream,
but I was awake. Eggy was there and so
was a DRAGON! I saw visions of the past.

When I took Eggy out of my pocket it was rumbling and glowing. I couldn't figure out why this was happening to me. It was supposed to be a rock!

"Oh, no! I think I need a nap!" I said out loud. As soon as we got home, I went straight to bed.

In my dream I was visited by the same dragon I saw earlier. She told me she needed my help. She lost something very special to her, a very long time ago.

She said to me "When a dragon has an egg, they must protect it and keep it safe. They must never be separated. If they do, they both turn to stone . . . forever."

Even worse, they eternally search for one another, so they can be at peace once again. Finally, now they were close enough to each other. That's why I felt the rumble when I held Eggy.

Before I woke up, she showed me her location. She mentioned that I had her egg and said, "You must bring Eggy to me."

When I woke from this dream, I
knew I had to find her and reunite
her with her egg.

When she showed me her location it looked like Dog Mountain, not too far from where I lived. It's called Dog Mountain because it sort of looks like a very big dog laying down.

"I've been by there so many times, and I don't remember ever seeing a dragon!" I said out loud to the mirror.

I got on my bike and
headed for school. Dog
Mountain was on the way.

"I will make a quick stop and be done with this. Everything will go back to normal." I reassured myself.

When I got there, the rumble was so strong. Eggy was practically pulling itself out of my pocket! I knew we were getting close.

The higher I
hiked toward the
center of Dog Mountain,
the fiercer the shake!
Now I could feel it under
my feet! It was getting
hard to walk and I was
starting to get a
little scared.

"Almost there, I have to
keep going." I muttered.

Just then I saw a glow coming from the side of the mountain. It was glowing in an egg shape. "That's got to be it!" I squealed. Eggy was almost jumping out of my backpack!

I pulled Eggy out. It was warm, bright, and humming in my hands. I was sad I had to let it go. I loved Eggy. I knew I had to do what was right. I placed Eggy into the center of the mountain where it was glowing.

Everything went quiet.
"That's it?" I spoke.

Then, suddenly A HUGE beam of light shot out of the top on Dog Mountain. A soft ghostly mist was lifting around me, and I could see it clearly now.

"It was never a dog! It's a
sleeping DRAGON!" I shouted.

Finally, they could rest. They would stay as precious stones forever. At last, they were together again!

As the mist started to fade you could see the Dragon cuddled into Eggy as if it were her baby. They were at peace.

"I did it!" I shouted.
In that bittersweet moment,
I knew I just had the
adventure of a lifetime!

THE END